JAMES IN SPACE
VOLCANOES OF VENUS

For Teegan and Tyrell.

First published in the UK in 2018
by New Frontier Publishing Europe Ltd
93 Harbord Street, London SW6 6PN
www.newfrontierpublishing.co.uk

ISBN: 978-1-912076-70-3

Text copyright © Candice Lemon-Scott 2015
Illustrations copyright © New Frontier Publishing 2015
Illustrations by Celeste Hulme
The rights of Candice Lemon-Scott to be identified as the author and
Celeste Hulme to be identified as the illustrator of this work have been asserted.

A CIP catalogue record for this book is available from
the British Library.

Printed in China
10 9 8 7 6 5 4 3 2 1

JAKE
IN SPACE
VOLCANOES OF VENUS

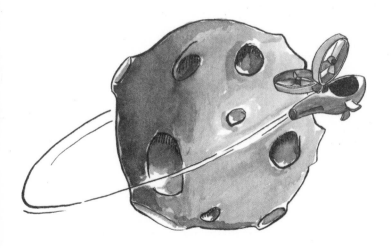

Candice Lemon-Scott
Illustrated by Celeste Hulme

Jake dropped his old backpack in amazement. He couldn't believe he was actually here at the Floating Hotel of Venus.

'Wow! This is the best prize ever,' a voice said.

Jake turned. It was Rory, who had just arrived from Mars with his mum and dad. And Rory was right – the hotel was even more incredible than Jake had heard. The foyer was round, with gleaming bronze pillars and walls that shimmered bright yellow like a golden waterfall. There was a flowing lava fountain in the centre of the room made from a shiny black rock. The floor was black too, and so shiny Jake could see his reflection in it. But there wasn't anyone to take them to their rooms. There was just a conveyor belt that ran all the way around the curved walls of the foyer.

Jake looked at his mum and dad standing beside him. Their mouths were open so wide they looked like they were trying to catch space bugs. A walking plant squelched past Jake. It reached out an arm and wrapped it around his mum's leg. She screamed and Jake's dad slapped the plant's arm away. It slunk away towards the entrance.

The front airlock doors slooped open again. This time Skye arrived with her mum. She said hello then walked straight over to the conveyer belt and placed her hand on a small white square on the wall. Her mum then did the same.

A smooth voice chimed through an intercom: 'Two guests. Room 3353. Thank you.'

Skye removed her hand and threw her bag onto the conveyer belt. Her mum placed hers down carefully. The bags moved along it until a small doorway opened up and the bags disappeared inside.

'How did you know to do that?' Rory gasped.

Skye pulled her notepod from her space suit pocket. A 3D image of the hotel foyer appeared. 'It's all right here. In the hotel guide,' she said, shaking her head.

Rory stared at her blankly.

'Go on! Try it.'

Rory picked up his bag and walked over to the shiny wall. He placed his hand on the square on the wall as Skye had done.

'Room 3352. Thank you.'

His bag was whisked away. Jake did the same and he was given Room 3354. Their parents nervously followed their lead. As the bags were taken Jake heard the front airlock sloop open once more. Milly came running in with her mum and stepdad.

'Phew,' she said, puffing. 'I thought we were late.'

'And you had such a long way to come,' Rory joked, knowing it would have only taken her ten minutes from her home in the neighbouring Floating City.

She poked her tongue out at him, then glanced down, looking at her reflection and posing in the cleaner-than-clean floor. 'I still can't believe we get to stay here!'

The Central Intergalactic Agency (CIA) had given Jake and his friends each a ticket after

they stopped thousands of remote-controlled robots from taking over the solar system at the Robot Games. It was the best gift *ever* for solving a mission! Only famous people stayed in this hotel. That reminded Jake that he hadn't seen Henry, the CIA's cyborg – and their friend – arrive yet. It wasn't like him to be late. Jake was about to mention it when Milly interrupted.

'Oooh, is that a lava fountain?' she cried and raced over to watch the red liquid spurting out of the fountain. She reached out to touch the oozing lava but then pulled her hand back sharply.

'Ouch! It's hot,' she cried.

'That's because it's lava, Milly!' Skye said. 'Are you okay?' She inspected her friend's hand.

'I'm fine,' said Milly. 'Look!' She pointed at the hotel's entrance.

The front doors slooped open again. Henry had finally arrived. He slowly made his way across the foyer, his shoulders slumped forward. He looked like a turtle with his silvery backpack for a shell.

'Good morning, Henry!' Jake said, cheerfully.

'Is it?' he grumbled.

'What's wrong?' Skye asked.

'Nothing,' Henry mumbled.

'Come on, Henry, just tell us,' Rory said, grumpily.

'I have been kicked out,' Henry said. 'They said I could go on a holiday.'

'That doesn't mean you've been kicked out,' Jake said.

'Cyborgs do *not* get holidays,' Henry insisted.

'Well, now that you have one you might as well have some fun,' Jake said.

'Yeah, let's go check out our rooms,' Rory agreed.

'Very well,' Henry said sadly, and moped over to the conveyor belt.

'How do we get to our rooms?' Jake asked, looking at Skye's notepod.

'Do you think we have to go up that stairway?' Rory asked.

Jake looked over to where Rory was pointing. A gigantic spiral staircase was at the far end of the foyer. But it was a staircase with no stairs – it was smooth, like a slide, and so high that Jake couldn't even see the top.

'I guess so,' Jake said, looking around at the

shimmering walls. 'I can't see an elevator or anything.'

'I can't imagine how we'd get up *there*,' Rory's mum commented, brushing down her neatly ironed suit.

They'd all been given special space suits to wear for the hot conditions on Venus. Jake looked down at his own suit. He had just thrown it on crumpled.

'What does your notepod say, dear?' Skye's mum asked in a soft voice.

Skye turned it this way and that, and then shrugged. 'I can't find anything. Maybe I can ask?'

'Ask?' Milly's stepdad said. 'There's no-one here to ask.'

Milly's mum nudged him in the ribs, whispering, 'Don't be rude.'

Skye walked over to a huge screen on the wall and said loudly, 'Activate.'

The screen lit up and the face of a beautiful woman appeared. She had a tight smile on her face as her lips curled back. She stared out from the screen and Jake noticed her irises were actually purple.

'Welcome to the Floating Hotel of Venus,' the woman said. 'I am your hostess, Valerie. I trust your stay will be enjoyable.'

Jake noticed her expression didn't change the whole time she was speaking. Her lips were smiling but her strange violet eyes weren't.

'How do we get to our rooms?' Skye asked.

'Please take the stairway.'

The screen went blank.

'That *is* the way!' Rory exclaimed.

'But how do we get up there?' Milly frowned.

Jake went over to the stairway to take a closer look. As he leaned forward and touched the smooth surface he felt a rush of warm air

10

and then *whoosh!* He shot up the stairway, twisting and turning as he was sucked straight along it. He was spat out at the other end so fast that he rolled along the ground. That was so much fun! He stood up and saw a large rock door. The number 3354 was burning like a candle on the front of it. He had to tell the others about this. He peered back down the stairway but he was so far up he couldn't see the bottom. He called down: 'Go up to the stairway! It'll take you to your rooms.'

Moments later his mum and dad slid off the stairway beside him. His mum patted down her hair as she stood up. 'Well, that wasn't the most graceful arrival,' she frowned.

'It was a lot of fun though,' Jake's dad replied, winking at Jake.

Jake's mum laughed. 'Yes, it was, wasn't it?'

'Do you have the key to our room, Jake?' his dad asked.

'Er, no …' he replied.

'Oh, then maybe a card?'

Jake realised he didn't have anything to get into the room. In fact, he couldn't see a keyhole, or even a card scanner. There was a small step attached to the door. He stood on it and brushed his hands over the door but nothing happened. Then he noticed a white square above him, like the one on the wall near the conveyer belt. He reached up and placed his hand on it.

Valerie's face appeared on the door. 'Welcome, Jake.'

The door turned, taking him with it until he was on the inside. He stepped off and the door revolved back again. Moments later his parents appeared next to him too.

The inside of their hotel room was even more amazing than the foyer had been. There were

12

velvet couches and a crystal table already set with shiny silver cutlery and bronze plates. In the centre of the room was a round, raised floor. There were two huge bedrooms, separated by a movable screen. On each wall was ever-changing scenery in 3D. A swirling mass of stars was shown.

'Wow! The Milky Way,' Jake exclaimed. 'It looks so real.'

'Doesn't it?' his mum replied, grinning. 'I wonder if there's a scene for Cancri.'

At that moment the scenery changed to show the diamond planet. It shone brilliant silver and was so bright that Jake had to cover his eyes.

'No way!' Jake cried. 'What about a black hole?'

The scene changed again. It was so realistic Jake felt like he was falling into the centre of the gap in space. Then he noticed a conveyer belt along one side of the room, appearing from one end and disappearing again at the other. On it was a non-stop supply of food, with every space snack Jake could imagine. There were glow cakes and jelly balls, honeycomb dipping fountains, Gob Pop and redesign biscuits that kept changing shape.

'Hungry?' his dad asked.

'You bet,' Jake replied, moving towards a teddy biscuit that had changed into the shape of a spider when he reached out to take it.

'You'd better wash your hands before you eat,' his mum said.

Jake sighed and opened the door to the bathroom, then gasped. The floor of the bathroom was completely clear. In a pool beneath his feet were tropical fish of every colour he could imagine. He lay down on the floor and watched them swim by, along with stingrays and even a sea turtle. When he

stood up he saw a huge bath in one corner. It was already filled with bubbling soapy water. He read the neon sign above the bath. It said the water in it was constantly reheated to the perfect temperature. He couldn't wait to try it out later.

He went over to the sink and washed his hands. As he went to dry them he found himself being sprayed by a fine mist. He sniffed and quickly started coughing. He had been sprayed with perfume! And it stank.

'Would you like lipstick applied?'

Jake jumped and looked around. Where had that voice come from? He peered into the mirror then stumbled back, nearly tripping over the sea sponge bathmat. Valerie's reflection was looking back at him.

'Er, no ... I don't want lipstick,' Jake said, startled. He already smelled like a girl.

'Voice recognition tells me you are not Lady

Marie?' Valerie said.

'Of course I'm not,' Jake huffed. '*Jake*. Room 3354.'

'Please scan your hand for identification.'

Jake looked around. He noticed the same kind of white panel by the door as he'd used in the corridor outside. He placed his hand on it.

'Welcome Jake,' Valerie said. 'Would you like some aftershave?'

'No thank you!'

Jake quickly opened the door and stepped out of the bathroom, slamming the door closed behind him.

His mum looked up, her mouth still fizzing from eating an exploding Fizz Flan. 'You look a little pale! Is everything okay?' she asked, bubbles of fizz escaping from her mouth as she spoke.

'Yeah,' Jake mumbled.

'Are you wearing ... *perfume*, Jake?' his dad asked, sniffing the air.

'No! I mean, I didn't mean to,' Jake stammered.

'It's okay, Jake,' his mum soothed. 'It's fine with us if you want to wear perfume. It is a little strong, though.'

Jake rolled his eyes then went over to the conveyer belt and picked up a pea-sized cream puff. The moment he put it into his mouth it puffed up into a fluffy cream cake. This was already turning out to be the best holiday ever. As he swallowed the puff there was a chiming sound at the door of their room.

'I wonder who that could be?' Jake's mum said.

'See who it is, will you, Jake,' his dad mumbled, his mouth full of honeycomb-dipped banana.

Jake raced to the door, expecting it to be

Rory. Instead, Henry was standing at the door, hopping from foot to foot. Before Jake could even say hello, Henry pushed the door open and slid past. He nodded at Jake's mum and dad and headed towards the small kitchen. He opened a rubbish chute beside the tiny sink. Even from where Jake was standing he could tell it really, really stank.

'Ewww, that's disgusting! I think someone's dumped rotten eggs in there,' Jake said, covering his nose. 'Close it up, Henry.'

But Henry just leaned forward, bent over the chute and had a big sniff.

'Henry!' Jake cried.

'That is not a rotten egg smell,' Henry said. He ran over to the door of the room, stood on the box and placed his hand on the sensor.

'Where are you going?' Jake cried.

But before Jake could get an answer out of him Henry had disappeared, the door

18

spinning closed behind him. Jake turned to his parents and shrugged.

'Your friend is a little odd, isn't he?' his mum said.

Jake met Milly, Skye and Rory in the foyer of the hotel the next morning. They had been booked on a special spacecopter tour of the volcanoes of Venus. It started in ten minutes.

'Where's Henry?' Skye asked.

Jake looked around the foyer. It was empty except for the four of them.

'I don't know,' Jake admitted. 'He went all weird last night. He came to my room, had

some strange idea, then left again. I was hoping he'd turn up for the tour.'

'I wonder if he's all right,' Milly said. 'He was pretty upset about the CIA not giving him a mission.'

'Yeah,' Jake agreed, 'but this was different. Henry seemed curious about something when he left.'

'You don't think he's got another mission, do you?' Skye asked.

'Not unless it's about rubbish,' Jake said.

Before he could explain any more, the foyer's screen lit up.

'Please make your way to the spacecopter. Your tour will begin in five minutes.'

When Jake stepped inside the spacecopter he couldn't believe what he was seeing. Henry was sitting in the pilot's seat.

'What are you doing here?' Jake cried.

'And where is our tour guide?' Rory added grumpily.

Henry held up a computer stick and gestured to the pile of metal lying crumpled in the back of the copter.

'The guide had a slight malfunction,' Henry grinned. 'Ready for the tour?'

'Are you serious?' Rory groaned.

'Strap yourselves in,' Henry beamed cheekily. He seemed to be out of his bad mood.

The ground beneath the copter fell away and they drifted down until they were below the hotel and the Floating City of Venus.

The spacecopter was soon enveloped in the heavy atmosphere of Venus. Outside the windows there was nothing to see except thick red cloud. It wasn't exactly the exciting tour Jake had expected after the fun of the

luxury hotel. Then, as they drifted lower, he saw the surface of Venus appear. There were hundreds of low-rising volcanoes covering it. Many were extinct but some had slow, sludgy flows of lava oozing from them, forming a blood-red maze of colour. Great plumes of smoke rose into the atmosphere. The rock around each volcano was as black as the night and shone with different patterns made by the hardened lava.

'I welcome you to the Volcanoes of Venus Tour,' Henry said in a posh accent.

The girls and Jake laughed and Rory just snorted. Henry flew over a large volcano, directly below the hotel.

'Wow! That's the Veno Volcano!' Skye said.

Rory pressed his nose against the window. 'No way!'

The volcano was like nothing Jake had ever seen before. It was bigger than all the others and thick smoky gas came up through different vents. With one hand on the controls, Henry pulled something out of his suit pocket. It was a small disc-shaped object.

'What's that?' he asked.

'It is a chemical sensor,' Henry said matter-of-factly.

'That's for measuring gas levels,' Skye said.

'That is right,' Henry said, sounding impressed.

'So you *do* have a mission?' Jake said, smiling. No wonder Henry was feeling happier.

'No!' Henry snapped.

'Then what are you doing with that thing?'

'I'm just curious about gas levels in the volcano.'

'You *really* don't know how to have fun,' Rory grumbled.

Henry ignored him. 'I just need to get this vehicle as close to the volcano as possible.

If you could please lower this down to the surface, Rory.' He handed Rory the sensor.

'Me?' he said.

'Yes, thank you,' Henry replied.

'Why do I always get the worst jobs?' he complained as he made his way to the back of the copter carrying the device.

Once they were close enough Rory opened the hatch. The smell of sulphur rose from the volcano, filling the copter.

'That stinks,' Milly cried.

'You'd better make it quick, Rory, before we all pass out,' Jake said, holding his nose.

'You should smell it from my end,' he groaned.

They watched as Rory lowered the sensor down. It landed on the surface. He started to undo the connecting cable as Henry instructed. Then the communications screen lit up and the face of Valerie appeared. She didn't look so friendly now as she scowled at them through the screen.

'You are in a restricted area. Please return to the tour route immediately.'

The screen went blank. Rory was still busy trying to detach the cable.

'We have to go. Now!' Jake said. 'Release the cable, Rory.'

Rory released it and the sensor landed on the side of the volcano. Henry handed Jake the computer stick from the robot pilot. Jake inserted it into the side of the crumpled robot's head. Straightaway the robot sprang into life and took over Henry's position in the pilot's seat.

'Welcome to the Volcanoes of Venus tour. Please be seated and buckle your belts.'

Jake wasn't sure what was worse – Henry hijacking the copter and getting them in

trouble or having the boring robot take them on the volcano tour right now. The robot droned on and on about the planet and described each volcano they flew over. Although the view was beautiful, the volcanoes looked pretty much the same after a while.

After they passed about the fiftieth one Jake thought he'd rather have his eyes gouged out than listen to the robot go on any longer. The others looked just as uninterested. Milly was plaiting her hair, Skye was playing a real reality game on her notepod and Rory seemed to be asleep. The moment the copter landed they jumped out. Henry was the quickest to unbuckle his belt and he raced through the doors as soon as they opened. He was in such a hurry he didn't notice he'd dropped something. Jake called out to Henry but he didn't hear him and soon disappeared. Jake picked up the object. It was a black box. He turned it over. It was totally plain and didn't look like it could do anything special at all.

'What's that?' Skye asked, leaning over Jake's shoulder.

'I don't know,' Jake replied. 'It's Henry's. I guess I'll just give it to him later.'

Jake put it in his suit pocket. He didn't think of it again until much later that night.

A loud beeping noise filled Jake's ears. He rolled over but the noise continued. He pressed his pillow over his head but he could still hear the annoying sound. Finally, he rolled from his softer-than-soft bed and landed on the warm, bouncy floor. Feeling around in the dark, Jake tried to follow the noise. The beeping got louder and louder until his hand touched the suit he'd been wearing the day before. The noise was coming from it. He pulled the beeping object from the pocket of his discarded suit. It was the black box Henry had dropped.

'Lights on,' Jake whispered.

Nothing happened.

'Lights on,' he said a little louder.

The light in his bedroom shone dully. He looked at the box. It was still beeping. Jake turned it over in his hands. He looked for a button or switch to turn it off but there was nothing. How was he going to make the noise stop? If he was going to get any sleep at all he had to find Henry. He was the only one who would know how to turn it off.

Jake slipped his suit on, wrapped the box in a towel and crept out of the room before his parents were woken too.

Once he was in the hallway Jake realised he didn't know which room Henry was staying

in. He decided to go to Skye's room – her room was the one next to his. If anyone could figure out where Henry was staying it would be her. The only problem was, he couldn't get in. He put his hand on the sensor but nothing happened. He pressed a buzzer but no-one answered. Just as he was turning to go the door swung open. A sleepy, grumpy-looking Skye appeared. She ran her hand through her ruffled hair.

'What are you doing here?' she whispered. 'It's the middle of the night!'

Jake held up the beeping parcel and quickly explained the problem.

'Wait here,' Skye grumbled. 'And keep quiet. You don't want to wake my mum and dad.'

She returned a minute later, holding her notepod. A miniature version of the hotel shone above the screen.

'How did you get a movement map?' Jake

said, 'Those were banned years ago.'

'You can still download them,' she said. 'You just have to know where to look.'

She scrolled through the rooms until a tiny version of Henry appeared. Jake could tell it was him straightaway from the stiff walk.

'Do you think he ever sleeps?' Jake asked.

'I don't know,' Skye answered, 'but he's definitely awake now.'

They followed the 3D map and headed down the empty corridor. They had reached the end of the hallway when Skye gestured for Jake to stop.

'We have to go down to the bottom level,' she said.

'Are you sure?' Jake asked.

'That's what the map says.'

The two travelled down to the bottom, below the hotel foyer, using the stairless stairway. Finally, they tumbled out the end and

looked around. They were in the basement. It was dark and dull compared to the rest of the hotel.

'This is it,' she said, pointing to the notepod.

Jake looked at the notepod, then looked up. 'This can't be it,' he said. 'Are you sure your notepod's working properly?'

'It says Henry's in here,' she answered.

'But this is the *basement*,' Jake argued. 'There has to be something wrong with the map. You don't really think he's in here, do you?'

'I don't know,' Skye replied. 'There's only one way to find out, though.'

They walked across the dim basement. It was hard to see where they were going in the dark and the smell was disgusting. Jake knocked into some old furniture and yelped as he hit his shin.

'Lights on,' Skye said. The lights flicked on.

33

'Wish I'd thought of that,' Jake grumbled, rubbing his shin.

There was no sign of Henry but Jake saw the basement was filled with rows of large bins. In one corner was a cleaning supplies cupboard. At the back were two huge doors with grates on them.

Jake went over to one of the bins and opened the lid. It was empty but there must have been some pretty revolting rubbish in there. The bin stank, worse than the time he forgot to put his sports socks in the wash for a week. He went over to another one of the bins. That one was empty too. As he walked around he realised all the bins were empty.

'Why do you think all these are here?' he asked.

Skye shrugged. 'They're just for rubbish. They've probably been emptied already.'

She walked over to the bins, lifted the lid

off one and poked her head in it.

'Ewww, that's revolting! I know it's a bin but it smells worse than mouldy cabbage.'

Jake heard a creaking sound. 'Shhh!' he whispered.

The door to the cleaning cupboard slowly opened. Jake put up his hands in a fight position even though he'd never done any boxing in his life. Someone jumped out of the cupboard. When he saw who it was he dropped his arms.

'Henry!'

'You scared me,' Skye yelled.

'Shhh!' Henry said. 'We can't talk here. Come with me.'

Jake and Skye followed Henry back to his room. Jake was dying to find out what the cyborg knew and what he had been doing in the basement. On the way, Jake passed Henry the beeping box.

'I am so pleased that you found it,' Henry whispered. He quickly unwrapped the towel, opened a secret compartment on the box and switched it off. Jake wished he'd known it was that easy to stop the annoying beeping.

Henry's hotel room looked similar to Jake's own room, only in Henry's there were machines everywhere. Henry attached the black box to one that was on the end of the table. He switched on another device and a clear glass screen popped up. A weird series of neon green lines started appearing on the glass. The lines were small at first but then grew larger.

'What are all those lines?' Jake said, slumping down on a squishy couch.

'They are showing the gas levels. The sensor we attached to the volcano is transmitting the data. As I thought, the levels are high and rising fast,' Henry said, as though it was the

most normal thing in the world to discover in the middle of the night. He pulled out the piece of glass and sat it on the table. He traced the lines with his finger, frowning.

'Huh?' Jake said. He turned to Skye. 'Do *you* know what he's talking about?'

Skye shook her head.

'High gas levels means the volcano is becoming more eruptive. It will be dangerously eruptive if they keep rising like this,' Henry said.

'Then what were you doing in the basement?' Skye asked.

'That smell coming from the bins is sulphur. I knew something must be wrong when I smelled the rubbish chutes, so I located the source of the odour last night,' he explained. 'The rubbish bins are collected by a flying rubbish truck.'

'There's nothing strange about that,' Jake said.

'No, but it did not answer my question about where the smell was coming from. So I jumped on the back of the truck. The rubbish was taken to the Veno Volcano. They are dumping the rubbish straight into it. That is where the sulphur smell is coming from.'

'That might not be the nicest way to dump rubbish, Henry,' Jake said, 'but what's that got to do with the volcano's gas levels?'

'I suspected the rubbish is somehow making the gas levels go up,' Henry explained, 'and I was right.'

Jake rolled his eyes. 'Volcanoes are full of gases.'

'No, the levels shouldn't change so quickly. I need to find out why.'

'So that's why you were hiding in the basement?' Skye asked.

'Yes, I needed to go out on the truck again, but then the two of you appeared instead.'

38

'I'm sure it's nothing, Henry,' Jake insisted. 'Maybe you should have tried getting some more sleep instead?'

'Well, I'm tired,' Skye said, yawning.

'Me too,' Jake admitted. 'We'd better go. Bye Henry.'

Henry waved a distracted goodbye as he looked at the gas readings again.

Jake and Skye wandered sleepily back to their rooms.

'Do you think Henry's right and there's something weird going on here?' Jake asked.

'I just think Henry's bored and needs a CIA mission,' Skye replied.

'I think you're right,' Jake agreed.

Skye was always practical and that made more sense than anything Henry had said. Jake said goodbye to Skye back at her door then sneaked back into his room.

Everyone staying at the hotel was gathered in the Main Hall for the famous Floating Hotel of Venus Great Feast. Jake's parents were the first to find their table. They sat up one end, where the adult meals would be served, while Jake and his friends found places at the other end. Jake watched as lava twirlers spun spirals of molten fire while jugglers tossed black volcanic rock spheres in the air. His mouth dropped open when he noticed hover trays filled with food begin

moving around the room toward the obsidian rock table they were sitting at.

Rory was the first to reach up and grab a plate filled with cakes and slices. Milly swiped a cupcake from Rory's plate.

'Wow! Glow cake,' she said.

'Hey! That's mine,' Rory complained.

Milly shoved the whole cupcake in her mouth. She swallowed and soon her stomach began to glow bright pink. She stood up and spun around, laughing.

'Wouldn't have wanted a pink glow anyway,' Rory shrugged.

Jake piled his plate high with super crunch biscuits and melt-in-your-mouth chocolates that really did melt in your mouth. Henry reached into a large bowl. When he pulled his hand back out his fist was full of Gob Pop. Jake grabbed Henry by the wrist before he could put any in his mouth. He reminded the cyborg how hooked he had been on the popcorn and how much trouble it had caused at the Robot Games.

'I don't want to see your stomach popping away like that *ever* again,' Jake said.

'Surely a few little pieces won't hurt?' Henry pleaded.

Jake shook his arm until Henry had let go of all of the Gob Pop. 'How about a fruit salad fruit instead?'

Jake put one of the oblong fruits in his own mouth. This one tasted like pineapple, strawberry and lime all mixed into one delicious flavour.

Behind a diamond-studded table at the front of the hall, the big screen lit up. Valerie appeared. She had that stuck-on smile on her face again.

'Please allow me to introduce you to the owner of the Floating Hotel of Venus, Mr Vince Vamoo.'

Jake couldn't help but notice the violet in her eyes flashed a darker purple when she said his name. He wondered if that smile was hiding something. No-one could hold a smile for that long normally.

The screen went blank again.

Jake strained to look at the table. He noticed there was a small man sitting in the centre of it. He stood and spoke into a voice projection box. His voice echoed around the room, bouncing off the walls so it could be heard by everyone.

'Welcome guests. As you would have already seen, we have the latest in hotel technology, not offered anywhere else in the solar system. Everything you'll find here is the latest design. I sincerely hope you have a most amazing time with us. I trust our lovely hostess Valerie is helping to make your stay wonderful. Please, enjoy the feast.'

The crowd clapped and cheered but all Jake could think about was that last comment about Valerie making everyone's stay wonderful. Thinking back to how her face had appeared when he was trying to use the bathroom, he wondered how she managed to look after all the guests – and do it with that smile on her face. The cheering stopped and Mr Vamoo sat down. The guests went back to the hover trays, piling their plates with food.

Soon everyone had squeezed in the very last crumbs they could fit into their now full stomachs. Milly was still glowing, Skye was looking green and Rory was leaning against Jake, too full to move. The only one who was doing anything was Henry. He was busy collecting dishes and scraping plates.

'Why is he cleaning up?' Milly asked.

'Yeah, that's more work than I've ever seen

Henry do,' Rory remarked.

Skye and Jake just looked at each other. They knew exactly what Henry was up to. He really did believe someone was mucking around with the hotel's rubbish removal.

'Let me take that,' Henry said to Rory, snatching the plate off him.

Henry marched off, scraps of leftover food piled up so high he could hardly see over the plates.

'That's strange,' Rory said. 'There's no way I'd do the dishes. Everything's done for you here.'

'It's not like him,' Milly agreed.

'He thinks something strange is going on with the rubbish,' Skye explained.

Jake looked over. One of the hotel guests was trying to dump her rubbish in the rubbish chute but Henry stopped her, taking the dirty plate. She walked off, looking worried. Jake knew they had to do something or Henry would end up being kicked out of the hotel. He left Skye to explain the whole story to Milly and Rory and walked across the room to Henry.

The hall was so full of guests eating, laughing and moving around that it took Jake at least two minutes of bumping into people to get across to Henry. By the time he reached the far side of the room, Henry had thrown a full bag of rubbish over his shoulder and was stamping out into the hallway, hunched over.

'What are you doing?' Jake said in his ear.

Henry jumped. 'N–n–nothing,' he said. 'I am just assisting with hotel clean-up.'

Jake frowned at him. That was the worst lie he'd ever heard.

'Then let me help too,' Jake said.

It wasn't until they had made it all the way to the basement with the smelly leftovers that

Jake realised what Henry was up to. Henry dumped the rubbish into the bins and then called loudly, 'Rubbish for removal.' He then motioned for Jake to hide in the cleaning cupboard with him. It was cramped in among the cleaning powders, mops and buckets but Jake did his best to keep still. He peered out of the cupboard. Before long the far doors in the basement opened up and a rubbish removal truck backed in. Robots emerged from the truck, loaded the full bins onto the back of it and flew out with their load. Once the doors had closed again, Jake and Henry stepped out.

'We have to find out what the rubbish is doing to the volcano,' Henry said.

He told Jake his plan. Jake's first thought was that it sounded like a really bad idea. If they got caught, they could get in a lot of trouble. His second thought was that it sounded exciting. He took a deep breath, and let it out again.

The words came out even before he could stop himself. 'Okay, I'll do it!'

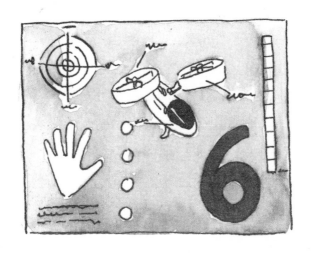

Minutes later, Jake left Henry in the basement, carrying the backpack Henry had given him. It didn't take long for him to find Skye, Milly and Rory. They had gone from the feast to the indoor theme park on the hotel's rooftop, where there were rides, games and simulators of all kinds. The friends were in the middle of a hover car battle, bashing into each other and trying to flip each other's cars in the giant games arcade. Jake flapped his arms at the edge of the games ring to get their attention.

'Where did you disappear to?' Skye asked Jake as she jumped out of her hover car. Milly and Rory followed.

'I can't say now,' Jake said quietly. 'But we need to go.'

'What, so we can lug around bags of rubbish with Henry? No thanks,' said Rory, but Skye gave him a nudge and they followed Jake out of the arcade.

Outside, Jake quickly explained what had happened, and how they were now going to take a spacecopter and follow the rubbish removal truck while Henry snuck on board the truck. That way he could find out exactly what was going on for himself.

'What?' Rory cried. 'You want us to *steal* a spacecopter? We don't even know how to drive one.' He started stomping back towards

the games arcade but Jake stopped him.

'We're just borrowing it. And it can't be that hard to drive. Henry did it. If we can drive a super-performance space car this should be a piece of glow cake.'

Rory looked to Milly and Skye.

'We *did* win the Rocket Battles,' Skye said.

'I think we can do it too,' Milly added.

Rory made a huffing noise. 'Why do I always get outvoted?'

When they got to the spacecopter hangar it looked like things were going to be even easier than Jake had first thought. The door to one of the copters was unlocked and there was no sign of the robot pilot. Rory took the pilot's seat. Milly switched on the controls and Skye brought up the navigation screen. Jake slid into position for front navigation. They were ready for take-off.

For a while nothing happened and Jake started to think Henry's plan wasn't going to work. Just as he was about to say they should just head back, the rubbish truck appeared. It was time to follow it.

'Accelerate – hard!' Jake told Rory. As he did, Jake realised this was probably a pretty bad idea after all. They really didn't have any idea how to fly the copter.

Rory took off. All of a sudden the copter began to spin, faster and faster. They began to fall down below the Floating City.

'I think I'm going to be sick,' Milly cried as she pressed buttons and turned dials.

Jake knew if they didn't figure out how to drive the copter soon they would crash onto the fiery surface of Venus. He navigated as best he could as Rory frantically steered and Milly tried every button on the copter's panel. Then they felt the copter stop spinning. It

wobbled and whirred. Moments later they were straight again.

'Look out!' Jake cried, 'Volcano to your left.'

'Going up,' Milly said, turning a dial.

'I think I'm getting the hang of this copter flying!' Rory said, grinning.

As the copter rose, Rory steered away from the volcano on their left but then nearly hit another on the right.

'Higher!' Jake yelled.

The copter rose even more and Rory flew over the volcano's peak. He and Milly finally had control of the machine.

'Where's the rubbish truck? I can't see it,' Skye said, sounding worried as she scanned the rear projection screen.

Jake squinted at his screen. 'It's to our left,' he said. 'The copter's drifted too far. Rory, we need to double back.'

Rory turned the copter around and headed

back towards the truck. It was moving towards the Veno Volcano. They followed and in a few minutes had reached the volcano.

The truck stopped above Veno's crater. The back doors opened up and a load of rubbish fell straight into the mouth of the volcano.

'It looks like they're just using it as a rubbish dump,' Skye said.

The truck flew off and the four got ready to return to the hotel. Skye stared at the rear projection screen.

Just as Rory was about to turn the copter around, Skye called out, 'Wait! There's something in the distance.'

Everyone looked through her screen. She was right. Something was flying towards the volcano.

'Quick! Let's get out of sight.'

Rory flew the copter down to the side of the volcano so they could be hidden. Through the

screens, Jake saw a truck come into view. It was identical to the other rubbish truck. This time, more than just rubbish was thrown in. Huge chunks of volcanic rock were emptied straight into the volcano.

'Where did that truck come from?' Milly asked.

'And why are *rocks* being dumped into the volcano?' Rory added.

'Maybe Henry's right. What if the gas levels are going up so high the volcano's getting dangerous?' Jake suggested. 'Maybe the hotel knows and is plugging it up so it won't erupt.'

'Like putting a lid on a super-fizz bottle,' Skye said.

'I hope it works,' Milly said. 'The Floating Hotel will be destroyed if the Veno Volcano erupts.'

'Yeah, no wonder they're doing it secretly. No-one would want to stay in a hotel with a volcano about to erupt underneath it,' Rory agreed.

Jake looked in the projection screen again. The truck was heading off, in the opposite direction to the hotel.

'Can we follow it?' Jake said.

'There's not enough fuel left,' Milly said, reading the controls.

'We'd better get back. Maybe we can check the gas levels again,' Skye said.

Jake sat in the jelly pond with Skye, Milly and Rory. He shoved a handful of bright green jelly in his mouth. Most of their parents were zooming overhead in the hover cars. Being such terrible drivers, Jake's parents kept bashing into everyone else. Jake looked down, embarrassed, as they flew too low and nearly hit Rory on the head. Meanwhile, Milly's mum and stepdad were dressed in reality suits and by the way they were walking they looked like they had just landed in quicksand.

'I wonder how Henry knew to check the gas levels,' Skye said, thoughtfully.

'I bet he *is* on a CIA mission,' Rory said.

'He seemed really upset when he said he thought he was being kicked out of the CIA though,' Skye said.

'Then why has he got all this gas-measuring gear?' Rory argued. 'It's not something you'd normally pack for a holiday, is it?'

'You know Henry. He probably just thought he could do some volcano research while he was here or something,' Milly said.

'I wish we could have followed the second truck that dumped all the rocks,' Jake said.

'Mmmm. It's a shame that copter didn't have more power,' Skye agreed.

As they were trying to figure it all out, Henry appeared. He squelched into the jelly

pond and sat down. He was holding the sheet of glass that had been in his hotel room, but now there were lots more green lines etched on it. He just about shoved it in their faces.

'This shows clearly that the gas levels have gone up,' he exclaimed.

'Wow, those levels really *are* going up,' Skye said as she examined the glass.

'I told you! Someone is sabotaging the volcano,' Henry stated. 'But there was only a robot on that truck. Someone else has programmed it.'

'Actually, we think someone's trying to save the hotel by stopping the volcano from erupting,' Skye said.

She explained to Henry what they'd discovered. The cyborg's eyes widened until they looked ready to pop straight out of his head.

'What's wrong, Henry?' Milly asked.

'A volcano works just like a super-fizz

bottle, like you said. By plugging it up the volcano cannot erupt. But it is also building up pressure in there.'

'What are you talking about?' Rory cried.

'Think of the volcano as a super-fizz bottle. The rocks are the lid. The volcano's gases are the bubbles inside the bottle. When you shake up the bubbles in a super-fizz bottle and then take off the lid, what happens?'

'It explodes everywhere,' Rory said.

'Yes, and I think that is exactly what they are planning to do here. They are going to build up the gases, then release the plug and BOOM, the volcano erupts!'

'How do you know that?' Rory scoffed.

'The gas levels are increasing, which means this volcano is nearly ready to blow.'

Everyone looked shocked. Everyone except Rory, who frowned like he'd just been told a bad joke.

'Did the CIA tell you that?' he grumbled.

'I'm sworn to secrecy,' Henry said, clamping his mouth closed.

Rory gave the others an I-Told-You-So look. Jake started to get annoyed. He'd thought Henry really was upset about not having a mission and had felt sorry for him.

'So you *do* have a mission,' he snapped.

'Okay, okay, I do,' Henry replied.

'That was mean, pretending you thought you were being kicked out.'

Henry looked surprised. 'No, that part was true. It was only when I contacted the CIA about the high gas levels that they gave me the mission –'

'We don't believe you,' Rory interrupted.

'It is true!' Henry cried.

'Then why do you have all that gas-measuring gear?'

'I am interested in volcanoes.'

Jake just frowned.

'Fine,' Henry said. 'I shall do this mission on my own. Your help will not be necessary anyway.' He wiggled his way out of the jelly pond and squelched away angrily.

Skye and Milly were glaring at the boys.

'What?' Jake said.

They crossed their arms. Jake knew they thought he had been a bit too hard on Henry. Maybe he had. Maybe Henry had stormed off like that because he *was* telling the truth after all.

Jake sighed. 'I'll go find him and say sorry,' he said.

'We're coming too,' the girls added.

'I guess I'd better come as well,' Rory groaned.

The four pulled themselves out of the jelly, then slipped and slid out of the arcade.

It wasn't hard to find Henry. He hadn't even bothered getting air-cleaned to blast the jelly off and had left a trail of wobbly globs in his path.

The jelly led them straight to the basement. When they got there Jake pushed the door. It was unlocked. They snuck in quietly. Henry didn't even notice they were there. He was too busy trying to open the door of the rubbish removal truck. He had his arm open, revealing the special control panel inside. He flicked out a tiny pick and quickly opened the driver's side door, then peered inside the truck.

'What are you doing?' Jake hissed.

Henry got such a fright he banged his head on the top of the door. Rubbing it, he turned around.

'Nothing,' Henry said.

'I'm sorry I didn't believe you before,' Jake

said. 'You just, well, you do have a habit of being secretive about the CIA missions.'

'That may be true,' Henry said slowly, 'but with feelings I am always truthful. I cannot lie about that. It is an unfortunate part of my make-up.'

Just then Jake heard a noise coming from outside. He could hear low voices and footsteps coming closer.

'Oh no!' Henry said.

'We don't want to get caught in here,' Skye said. 'We'll get kicked out of the hotel for sure.'

Jake agreed, thinking back to how angry Valerie had been when they got busted taking over the copter. He heard the voices getting louder. The footsteps stopped then began again. Jake heard a woman's voice. She was saying something about the jelly footprints. It sounded like Valerie's voice. Then a man began arguing with her – it was Vince Vamoo, the hotel owner. There was movement. The

voices sounded very close now.

'What are we going to do?' Milly whispered.

Henry pointed to the bins.

'You can't be serious?' Rory hissed. 'That will never work!'

'You won't be in there long,' Henry insisted.

'I don't think we've got much choice, unless you want to get caught,' Jake said. 'There's no other way out.'

Jake sped over to one of the empty bins. He lifted the lid, climbed inside and closed the lid again. It was dark in there and smellier than if he'd had his dirty sports socks shoved up his nose. He tried not to inhale the smell but it was impossible. He tried breathing through his mouth but the smell was all around him. *I hope I don't have to be in here for too long*, Jake thought. He wondered whether it was possible to die from inhaling too many disgusting smells.

Jake heard the lids close on four more of the bins as Rory, Milly, Skye and Henry climbed into one each. The basement door creaked open and the voices they'd heard before got louder. Vince was talking to Valerie.

'Take this rubbish away immediately,' he shouted.

'Yes, Vince,' Valerie said in a quiet voice.

'I don't want to see any more mess like I found in the hallway,' Vince said. 'All rubbish is to go straight into the volcano like I ordered.'

The door slammed closed, sounding as though Vince had left the basement. Jake could hear Valerie mumbling under her breath. No wonder she wasn't happy, especially with the way Vince had spoken to her. He felt a little sorry for her. But right now he was a bit more worried about how stinky the bin was, and how he was starting to cramp up. It would be terrible if they got caught hiding there.

Jake heard Valerie shuffling around and he wondered what she was doing. There were footsteps and then nothing for a few seconds. The next thing he knew the bin he was in was tipped on its side and he was being rolled somewhere. He heard the thump of other bins being tipped and rolled too. He bit his lip to stop himself from yelling out. He didn't want to get caught now. How would he explain being hidden inside a bin or why he'd been in the hotel basement to begin with?

Then he stopped rolling and the bin was pulled upright again. He heard the sound of an engine starting. *Oh no! I'm in the rubbish truck!* he thought. He felt the truck take off, his friends and him still hidden inside the bins. Jake knew they were in real trouble now. The truck was heading to the Veno Volcano and they were about to be thrown in.

efore long, Jake felt the flying truck come to a stop. He could hear some noises, then a thump. He wanted to push the lid off the bin and see what was going on but he knew it was too risky. He'd just have to wait to see what was happening. Was it suddenly hotter? He felt the bin move. *Uh-oh!* Jake really *really* hoped he wasn't about to be burned alive. He was tipped over again and he felt the bin being rolled once more. He was sure he was about to be thrown into the

volcano with the rest of the rubbish.

But then he stopped rolling. The lid of the bin was pulled off. Jake looked out and saw the smiling face of Henry. He slowly crawled out and blinked, letting his eyes adjust to the light. Skye, Milly and Rory climbed out of their bins.

'Where are we?' Rory asked.

They were inside a huge room. Its walls were shining the deepest of black – they were entirely made of obsidian rock. The room itself looked like some kind of laboratory. There were reflecting obsidian screens with neon laser lights moving up and down and in all directions. There were self-writing pens recording information on a drawing panel and all kinds of glass jars full of strange liquids and powders. There was something bubbling inside a huge vat and empty canisters were lined up on a bench. Jake heard footsteps.

'Valerie must have brought the bins here to fill them with the rocks to throw into the volcano,' Henry whispered. 'Quick! We have to hide.'

Not again, Jake thought.

There was a small door at the far end of the lab. Jake and his friends raced over, opened the door and hid inside the room. It was dim and freezing, and Jake started to shiver. He realised they must be in a storage coolroom. Containers lined the shelves. He was about to lead the others back out when he heard someone enter the lab. It was too late to hide somewhere else. Great! He was trapped in some weird science lab in a freezing cold room with a madwoman outside. This was exactly the opposite of what he should be doing – having fun at the Floating Hotel of Venus. At least he hadn't been burned alive in the volcano.

Jake peeked through the small window in the door, standing on his tiptoes to see out. He could see Valerie. She was standing beside a robot. They were both dressed in lab coats and were wearing eye-protection glasses. But what was she doing here and what did the chemistry lab have to do with anything?

Jake turned to tell the others what he could see. Skye's teeth were chattering. Milly was rubbing her arms to keep warm and Rory was bouncing on the spot. Jake hoped they wouldn't be stuck in here for long. He peeked out of the window again. The robot went over to the bench, carrying a canister. It filled the canister with some powder and cupfuls of gooey-looking liquid then put a cap over the canister and put it aside. It went to fill another one but this time it seemed to have run out of the powder. It was showing the empty container to Valerie. She went over to the robot. Jake couldn't hear what was being said but Valerie looked angry and was waving her hands in the air. The robot followed Valerie out of the room. Now was their chance to escape.

Jake tried to open the door but it was stuck tight. He pulled harder but still the door wouldn't budge. He called Henry over. With his cyborg strength, if anyone could open the door it would be him. But even Henry couldn't open it. Jake shivered again. What were they going to do? They were trapped and the options weren't good. Even if they got out, who knew what Valerie and her robot scientist would do to them? But if they stayed in the coolroom for much longer they'd freeze to death. Jake started to wonder how long it would take to die from the cold. Or would they die from starvation first? He remembered back to the survival training

they had done at school. Wasn't it only three days you could survive without water?

Skye felt around the walls of the room. 'There's no other way out of here,' she announced.

'Maybe we can smash the window?' Rory suggested.

Jake looked around the dim room. 'There's nothing to do that with,' he said.

Now he could see better in the dark he could read some of the labels on the containers: 'Motor oil', 'Binder', 'Plasticiser'.

'What's all this for?' he asked.

'It is the material needed to make explosives,' Henry explained. 'I suspect that is what they are doing in the lab.'

'They're making bombs?' Milly screeched.

Henry nodded slowly.

'So they're planning to blow up the volcano?' Jake cried.

'And once the rubbish and rock plug is blown apart the volcano will erupt,' Henry said.

Jake wished he'd listened to Henry earlier. Now they were stuck in here and they couldn't do anything to stop Valerie.

'What are we going to do?' Milly cried.

'We shall need to conserve energy until a solution is found,' Henry said.

Rory started to yell at him for his unhelpful advice but it was too late. Henry had shut himself down.

Jake and his friends sat down and huddled together in a corner to keep warm. They would just have to wait and hope someone found them, even if that someone was Valerie.

Later, when Jake was so cold he couldn't feel his fingers or toes, he heard a noise. He told Rory to switch Henry back on.

'Do we have to?' Rory moaned before going over to the cyborg.

He reluctantly switched him on and Henry's eyes flicked open.

'Huh? Where are we?' he said.

Jake reminded Henry what was happening then stood up and shuffled over to the window. He looked out.

'What can you see?' Milly asked.

Jake saw the robot walking in their direction. It was carrying an empty container.

'The robot's heading this way.'

Henry picked up a container marked 'Plasticiser'. He motioned for the others to stand back. The robot came up to the door and opened it. The moment it saw Henry and his nearly frozen friends, it stepped back, turned and yelled.

'Intruder alert! Intruder alert!'

Henry took his chance and hit the robot

over the head with the container. The robot stumbled in a circle, dazed. Jake and his friends ran out, past the robot. They raced across the room towards the entrance. When Valerie saw what was happening her mouth opened in a soundless scream. She finally found her voice and yelled at the robot.

'Get them, you idiot!'

Regaining its balance, the robot raced towards them with Valerie not far behind. Jake wrenched open the door to the lab.

'Quick! To the rubbish truck!' Henry yelled.

The only problem was, none of them knew where the truck was because they had been dumped inside the lab while they were still hidden inside the bins. Jake hoped Henry knew what he was doing. The cyborg looked left and right. The lab opened into a long, empty hallway running in both directions. Henry turned left. Jake followed. He didn't

have much choice but to hope Henry could find a way out of this place. Everyone's feet clunked against the grated floor as they ran with the robot close behind. Valerie's voice echoed down the hallway.

'Get them! Get them!' she screamed at the robot.

Jake looked over his shoulder. Valerie and the robot were quickly gaining on them. If they didn't make it out of this place soon they'd be caught. Jake's heart was pumping hard but he kept on running. Up ahead he could see a door. He hoped it was a way out. It was their only chance. Henry reached the end of the hallway and pushed the door open. They stepped through into a huge hangar. It too was made from shiny black rock. Inside were two rubbish trucks. They piled into the back of one of them. Henry took the driver's seat.

'Do you know how to fly this thing?' Rory said, skidding into the co-pilot seat.

'I am programmed for flying many different vehicles,' Henry replied.

'Phew!' Skye said, taking up the rear navigation.

'A rubbish truck is not one of them but I think I can figure it out,' Henry added.

'Great,' Rory moaned.

Jake sat in the front navigation position.

Milly looked over the controls. 'I don't even know which button will start it.'

'You'd better find out quickly,' Skye said. 'The robot and Valerie are right behind us.'

Milly pressed a couple of buttons but nothing happened. Then she saw a huge black one in the middle of the controls and tried that. The truck made a whirring sound.

'They've reached the truck,' Skye cried. 'Lift off, lift off!'

Jake looked in Skye's screen. She was right. The robot had grabbed hold of the back of the truck. It was still holding on as they started lifting off the ground. Through Skye's screen, Jake could see its metallic fingers wrapped around the rear bumper.

'Higher!' Jake screamed.

The truck shifted upwards and the robot's fingers disappeared. That was close!

They flew out of the hangar. Jake looked through the front projection screen. He had no idea where they were but he knew they had to head back to the hotel, and fast. They had to warn everyone before Valerie blew up the volcano. As they rose above the lab, Jake saw that they'd been inside a huge black castle. It looked like something out of a horror story. It was all dark and gnarly-looking with jagged pieces of rock poking out everywhere. There were no windows. It had an evil-looking tower on top, like the one fairytale princesses got locked inside. In the centre there was a tall spire of rock with a blood-red flag flying from the top in a large 'V'. 'V' for Valerie, Jake guessed. And they were about to fly over it.

'Whoa! Lift, lift,' he screamed.

Henry shot upwards. Jake heard the sound of metal scraping, like a train screeching to a stop. The underside of the truck had hit the point of the flagpole on top of the spire.

'Sorry!' Jake muttered.

He glanced over to see Milly frantically pushing buttons.

'Oh no!' she exclaimed.

'What is it?' Jake cried.

'We must have hit the fuel tank,' she said. 'The levels are falling. Fast.'

'What do we do?'

'I don't know!' Milly replied.

'Do we have enough to make it back to the hotel?' Rory asked.

'We don't even know where the hotel is from here,' Jake said.

'Um, guys,' Skye interrupted. 'We have another problem. Valerie and the robot have followed us in the other truck. And they're gaining on us.'

'I have a solution,' Henry said. 'Rory, you take over the driving.'

'That's right,' he moaned. 'Get me to drive when we're running out of fuel and we're about to be caught by the baddies.'

'Okay then,' Henry said. 'You go out there and plug up the fuel tank and I'll drive. See how you go trying to do that, human.'

Jake couldn't help laughing. Rory looked more surprised than if he'd just found out someone had put space bugs in his sandwich. But Jake kind of liked this new Henry, who had stood up for himself for the first time ever. He looked back at Henry. A plunger that looked like something you'd stick down a toilet was poking out of his arm.

'I will plug up the hole with this,' he stated.

'Is that going to work?' Skye asked.

'There is only one way to find out the answer to that question,' Henry replied.

They flew across Venus with Henry attached to the fuel tank on the bottom of the truck. Valerie's truck followed close behind. None of them had a clue where they were. Jake thought they were either going to be captured by Valerie or run out of fuel, lost in space forever. He wasn't sure which would be worse.

Jake stared into the front projection screen as they continued flying across the surface of

Venus. Then he saw it. The Veno Volcano.

Valerie wasn't far behind. They were never going to make it back to the hotel.

'They've almost caught up,' Skye cried. 'Can you go any faster, Rory?'

'I'm on maximum speed,' he replied.

'Wait! I think I've found the boosters,' Milly said.

She pressed a button on the huge control panel. The truck lurched forward then stopped for a second. Jake began to think they were definitely doomed. Then he was thrown back as the truck shot forward.

'You did it!' Jake cried.

Milly smiled as Rory swerved right around the volcano and then shot upwards. The hotel came into view. Then Skye screamed.

'They're right on our tail,' Skye exclaimed. 'They're using their boosters too.'

Just as the words left her mouth the truck

jerked and shuddered.

'What's happening?' Milly yelled out.

Jake and Skye both stared into their screens helplessly.

'I can't see anything,' Skye said.

But Jake could. Valerie's car had slipped in front of them. And she had thrown out a tow winch that hooked onto their truck. It was pulling them up, up, up. They'd been caught.

Jake and his friends were towed back to the castle and thrown inside Valerie's lab once more. She'd told the robot to tie them all up so they couldn't get away again. The robot had even found Henry, still clinging on to the bottom of their truck. Jake tried to pull free from the ropes but it was no use. They weren't going anywhere, and with Valerie guarding them there was nothing the kids could do to alert everyone about what

she was planning. The robot was busy making the last of the explosives while Valerie stood over the five friends.

'Who are you and where did you come from?' Valerie demanded.

That stuck-on smile was still on her face, even though she spoke angrily and her eyes glowed deep purple.

'We're just hotel guests,' Milly stammered.

'I don't like guests who mess up my plans,' Valerie snarled.

'Plans to make the volcano erupt?' Skye screeched.

'How did you know about that?' Valerie said, looking surprised even though she was still smiling.

'You'll never get away with it!' Jake screamed.

'Who's going to stop me?' she grinned. 'Soon the explosives will be dropped into Veno. Once the plug is blasted apart the volcano will erupt and the Floating Hotel will be destroyed.'

It was just as Henry had said. Once the lid was off the volcano there would be a giant eruption.

'Why would you destroy the hotel you work at?' Milly pleaded.

'Because, my dear, I do all the work at the hotel while Vince gets all the thanks for it.'

'But you'll be out of a job,' Jake said.

'I was the one who created the hotel in the first place, until Vince took over,' she snapped. 'I should be running it, not working in it.'

'You can't do that if it's destroyed,' Skye argued.

'No, but I will be the new owner of the Hidden Hotel of Venus. And this time it really will be my hotel and no-one will be able to take it over.' Valerie threw her head back and laughed.

'You don't mean this ugly castle ...' Milly began.

'This is the castle I built, with a little robot help!' Valerie barked. 'Don't upset me or I might just throw you into the volcano myself.'

'Our parents will be looking for us by now. We've been gone for hours,' Skye said.

'Oh, don't worry your pretty little head about that. I programmed in a special hotel announcement on the way back to the castle. You're taking part in the hotel games afternoon.'

Jake sat there silently, trying to think of a way to stop Valerie but he didn't have any ideas. Only minutes later the robot finished making the explosives. There was no time left.

'Now, back to the hotel and Vince will never suspect it's not just a normal rubbish-dumping day.'

Valerie marched the tied-up kids back to the truck. The robot clomped along behind, carrying the explosives. They were all doomed!

Valerie flew the truck back to the hotel, landing at the basement. The robot opened the back hatch of the truck and carefully carried the explosives out. Jake watched helplessly from the back of the truck.

'Set the explosives to go off,' Valerie said, holding out her hand to the robot.

The robot punched some numbers into a device Valerie was wearing like a watch. Then the robot put the explosives inside some of the empty bins and topped them with rubbish. It replaced the lids and carried the bins back onto the truck, sitting the ticking bombs right in front of Jake and his friends.

Valerie looked at the device strapped to her wrist. 'In just twenty minutes I will be the new hotel owner for the planet Venus. I have just enough time to collect my belongings before leaving this horrible place forever.'

She turned to go, ordering the robot to follow her.

'You can help me carry my things to the truck,' she said.

The minute she was gone Henry sprang into action. Little did Valerie know one of them was a cyborg. He flicked open the control panel in his arm and a tiny saw popped out. He cut his ropes with it and then his cyborg fingers moved faster than a space race car as he expertly undid the rest of the ropes. Jake felt his hands come free. He shook them and jumped to his feet.

'What now?' Milly asked.

Jake had an idea. He raced over to the hotel's cleaning cupboard and pointed to the tubs of powder lining them.

'How is that stuff going to save us?' Rory groaned.

Jake quickly explained. They'd have to act fast if his plan was going to work.

Everyone agreed it was the only way.

Once they were done carrying out Jake's plan, Henry tied the five of them back together, leaving the knots loose so they could escape later. Just as Henry tied himself back in the circle the basement door opened.

Valerie peered into the back of the truck and saw them all tied together exactly as they'd been before she left. She was wearing a long dress, the same shiny black as the ugly castle. It covered her whole body except her hands and face. She wore lipstick and nail polish to match. Her white skin glowed sinisterly against the dark colours.

'Still here I see,' she said, laughing at her own joke. She didn't suspect a thing.

The robot entered the truck, its arms loaded

with boxes holding her belongings.

'Set it down there,' she ordered, 'and let's go destroy this place.'

Moments later the truck took off. They were headed for the Veno Volcano. Jake felt more nervous than he had lining up to begin the Rocket Battles race. They stopped above the mouth of the volcano and Valerie started ordering the robot about. It lifted a bin and frowned. It put it down again. Jake tried not to react but he started to worry that the robot knew something was wrong.

'What are you doing?' Valerie screeched. 'Get a move on.'

'There is a problem,' the robot said.

Jake caught Skye's eye. She looked scared, just like he felt. If Valerie found out now what they'd done they would probably become the next lot of rubbish to be thrown into the volcano.

'What problem?' Valerie said.

'The lid is not sealed shut,' it said.

'Oh, you silly fool,' Valerie cried. 'What does it matter? The whole lot is going in anyway.'

'There's something else that ...'

'Just throw it in or *you'll* go in the volcano,' Valerie snapped.

Jake could guess what the robot had been about to say. Being computer-programmed it would have sensed that the bin was too light. It was just lucky Valerie was so impatient.

The robot threw the first bin into the

volcano. It did the same with another. While Valerie jumped up and down with glee, clapping her hands like a little kid as she watched the bins drop into the volcano, Henry slipped to the front of the truck. In a flash he was back, tying himself into the circle behind the last few bins.

'In five minutes the bombs will go off, the volcano will erupt and the Floating Hotel will be no more,' Valerie said as the last bin fell.

She commanded the robot to fly them back to the castle.

'I'd better get the new improved hotel ready for my guests. We don't want them having nowhere to go once the horrible Floating Hotel is burned to a crisp now, do we?' she laughed, sitting down beside the robot. She turned to Jake and his friends. 'And look! I even have my first guests.'

She laughed her horrible laugh again. Jake

felt his tummy turn to molten lava like the volcano. If they didn't stop Valerie in time their parents would all be trapped inside the burning hotel. He looked at his friends. They looked just as worried and scared as he felt. He knew he needed to keep calm though. If not, he wouldn't be able to think clearly enough to carry out his plan and outsmart Valerie.

The robot tried to start the truck's engine but nothing happened. It pressed buttons on the control panel but all that could be heard was a low hissing sound.

'What's the hold-up?' Valerie snapped. 'Get moving or we'll all go up in flames.'

'There is a problem with the power,' it said.

'Well, fix it. NOW!'

The robot pressed the same buttons again. Still nothing happened. Jake knew he couldn't show how nervous he was. He didn't want Valerie to suspect they had anything to do with the engine failure. He looked out through the rear projection screen. Stars shone red, like tiny rubies. It would be pretty if he wasn't so busy thinking about how they'd all die a fiery death if the plan didn't work. The five of them listened in as Valerie kept yelling at the robot.

'Um, excuse me,' Jake interrupted.

'What?' Valerie snapped.

'There seems to have been an engine failure,' he said.

'I can see that,' Valerie said angrily. She looked at her watch. 'It's only two minutes and forty seconds until the explosives go off!'

'I guess you'd better send your robot out to fix the engine now or we'll all be blown to bits,' Jake said.

'Get out there and see what the problem is!' she shouted at the robot.

The robot blinked and moved past the kids to the back of the truck. Valerie started pacing

up and down nervously. The robot opened the back hatch. Now it was Henry's turn to play his part. As the robot went to step out, Henry pulled his arms loose from the ropes and grabbed the robot by the leg. Henry swung the robot around above his head. Seeing what was happening, Valerie raced to the back of the truck.

'Noooooooooooooo!' Valerie cried.

She was too late. Henry let go of the robot and it flew out of the truck, disappearing into the open mouth of the volcano. Valerie's eyes glowed angrily.

'That robot weighs nearly a tonne,' she screamed at Henry. 'What are you?'

'I am Henry,' he said simply. 'I am a cyborg and I have the starter for the engine.' He held up the engine part.

'It was you that sabotaged the engine?' she cried and looked at her watch, panicking. 'But we only have one minute until eruption.'

'Then you had better let us take control of this truck,' Henry said, holding the starter in her face. 'Does everyone agree?'

On cue, Jake pulled free from his loose ropes. Milly, Skye and Rory did the same. Valerie looked even whiter against her black gown.

'Okay, okay. Just get me out of here before the volcano erupts.'

'We'd better tie you up. We don't want *you* trying to get away,' Jake said.

Valerie growled but she didn't struggle when Milly and Skye grabbed her by the arms and tied her tightly in the same ropes she'd used to capture them.

'Ten seconds until eruption,' Henry said as he put the starter back in. Instead of taking off, he hovered above the volcano.

'Nine, eight, seven ...' Jake and his friends continued.

'Hurry you fools!' Valerie yelled.

'Two, one ...'

'Nooooooooooooooo!' she screamed.

The friends just smiled at each other as nothing happened.

'The volcano didn't erupt,' Valerie barely whispered. 'You tricked me, but how?'

'It was your plan. Why don't you tell her?' Henry said to Jake.

Jake quickly explained that Henry had cut them free from their ropes back at the hotel. He told her how they had swapped the explosives for cleaning powder from the cupboard then covered it with rubbish again. Henry dismantled the explosives that were now safely locked inside the cleaning cupboard. They had then pretended to be tied up again. Finally, Henry had taken the engine starter from the front of the truck so Valerie would think they were all about to be blown up and would do what they wanted.

As Jake happily finished telling Valerie how there wasn't going to be any eruption, he heard the sound of a space car. He looked in the projection screen. A familiar sleek, silvery vehicle appeared.

'Just in time,' Jake said.

Minutes later the CIA agents Bree and Will boarded the truck. There was another agent with them as well. The short woman was loaded with bags and briefcases, her face redder than Mars as she climbed in behind them.

Will turned to the female agent. 'Did you remember the cuffs, Junior?'

'Of course,' she smiled.

'Get them out then,' he scowled.

The agent fumbled with the bags and Jake felt sorry for her. It didn't look like it was much fun being a junior agent in the CIA.

While she was busy dropping the cuffs and trying to pick them up again, still holding the cases, Bree looked at the captured Valerie and smiled.

'Thank you for the alert, Henry. We got here as quickly as we could,' she said.

'But it looks like you had it all tied up anyway,' Will added.

The friends tried to hide a groan.

'Even I know that is a terrible joke,' Henry said.

Bree and Will got Junior to cuff the screaming Valerie and load her onto the CIA space car. The agents were busy thanking Jake and his friends for their work when a sulking Junior returned.

'She's safely on board, boss,' Junior said.

Will nodded back at her sharply.

'Great job, crew,' Bree said to Jake and his friends. 'Now there's just one thing left to do.'

Bree opened up her briefcase and pulled out a diamond drill. She handed it to Junior, who turned it over in her hands, frowning.

'You will need to drill holes in the sides of the volcano to let out some of the pressure slowly. Then we can pull the rock plug out with the CIA car super claws when it's safe.'

'Oh, but, ah, isn't that a bit dangerous … for me?' Junior cried.

'Nothing is too dangerous for a CIA agent,' Will snapped. 'We'll drop you at the side of the volcano.'

Junior grumbled and took the drill, making her way slowly to the space car.

Bree turned to Jake and his friends. 'Thank goodness you figured out what Valerie was up to. We thought it was Vince Vamoo trying to sabotage the volcano.'

'Yes, we'll make sure you get something special in return for your efforts,' Will added.

'Why was he even throwing rubbish into Veno?' Jake said.

'Yeah, it's a pretty stupid thing to do if you ask me,' Rory agreed, 'He could have blown himself up.'

'Yes, Vince Vamoo's plan to get rid of hotel rubbish cheaply by throwing it in the volcano backfired,' Bree explained. 'It seems our Venusians need to be taught about the dangers of reckless waste disposal.'

'We'll be in touch,' Will said. 'Have fun!'

Henry waved goodbye too and turned to follow the agents to the car.

'Where do you think you're going?' Will asked.

Jake saw Henry's face turn blank. Had he been right? Was his friend really being kicked out of the CIA after all?

'I thought ...' Henry began.

'You thought wrong,' Will said, then his face

broke into a smile. 'You'd better finish your holiday with your friends before you even think of coming back to work.'

Henry smiled back and sat down in the truck again.

Once the agents had flown off the five friends took their positions back in the rubbish truck. Milly switched on the flight controls and Rory and Henry flew them back to the hotel with Skye and Jake navigating.

They pulled in awkwardly to land, then ran all the way down the corridors to the games arcade. Their families were sitting together and jumped up the minute they saw the kids.

'You were gone so long,' Jake's mum cried. 'We were starting to get worried about you all.'

'Ah, it was a pretty long game,' Jake answered, smiling.

The others all laughed. It sure had been.

ABOUT THE AUTHOR

Candice enjoys writing stories about turbo space cars, hurtling asteroids and evil villains. Her quirky style, fast-paced narratives and originality appeal to reluctant boy readers in particular.

Following several years working in the media, Candice now devotes her time to her writing and to raising her two daughters.